# Michael Bird-Boy

story and pictures by

Tomie dePaola

**Simon and Schuster Books for Young Readers** • Published by Simon & Schuster Inc., New York

To Boss-Lady

Simon and Schuster Books for Young Readers
Simon & Schuster Building
Rockefeller Center
1230 Avenue of the Americas
New York, New York 10020

Copyright © 1975 by Tomie dePaola

Published by the Simon & Schuster Juvenile Division
SIMON AND SCHUSTER BOOKS FOR YOUNG RE.
is a trademark of Simon & Schuster Inc.

Manufactured in the United States of America

10  9  8  7  6  5  4  3  2

10  9  8  7  6  5  4  3  2  (pbk)

Library of Congress Cataloging in Publication Data

dePaola, Thomas Anthony, 1934–
    Michael Bird-Boy
    SUMMARY: A young boy who loves the countryside
determines to find the source of the black cloud
that hovers above it.
    [1. Pollution—Fiction]    I.  Title.
PZ7.D439Mi  [E]    74-23563
ISBN 0-671-66468-9
ISBN 0-671-66469-7 (pbk)

Michael Bird-Boy lived in the country.

Every day was the same. He woke up and washed his face.

He put on his bird suit and ate his breakfast.

Then Michael Bird-Boy did his work. At night, he sat down and looked at the stars.

And every day was different.

The sky and the leaves were always different.

But one day was very different. A black cloud came across the sky.

And when night came, Michael Bird-Boy couldn't see the moon or the stars.

The white birds were dirty. The flowers wilted.

So he packed his suitcase,

and went off to find what was causing the black cloud.

He walked and walked until he came to the city.

And there he saw it.

"Hi, I'm Boss-Lady," said a voice. "Do you want a job in my factory?"
"I'm Michael Bird-Boy," said Michael, "and I live in the country. Your black cloud is making the white birds dirty and the flowers wilt. We can't even see the moon and the stars at night."

"Well, Mike," said Boss-Lady. "I'm sorry. I make Genuine Shoo-Fly Artificial Honey Syrup in my factory from  tons of sugar and artificial honey flavoring. It's great on pancakes. But I guess that melting all that sugar in the big furnace makes  a lot of black smoke."

"Why don't you make real honey?" asked Michael Bird-Boy. "Bees don't make smoke."

"Gee, Mike, what a great idea," said Boss-Lady. "Where can I get some bees?"

"I'll send you some," said Michael Bird-Boy.

So Michael Bird-Boy went back to the country and sent Boss-Lady some bees. She shut off her furnace and started to make real honey.

...e white birds were white again, the flowers weren't wilted anymore,
...d Michael Bird-Boy could see the stars and moon at night.

One day the telephone rang. "Hello Mike, this is Boss-Lady. I have a terrible problem. Your bees aren't working."

So Michael Bird-Boy went all the way back to Boss-Lady's factory.
She was waiting for him. "Come inside," she said.

"Look! No honey!" she said pointing to the rows of empty jars.
"The bees are just sitting there buzzing!"

"I planned it so carefully," she said. "Look at my charts!"
Michael Bird-Boy looked.
"Where are the flowers?" he asked.

"Flowers?" said Boss-Lady.
"Bees need flowers and hives," said Michael Bird-Boy.

And he drew a picture to show Boss-Lady how bees make honey. "No wonder no honey," said Boss-Lady. "Thanks again, Mike."

A few weeks later Michael Bird-Boy got a letter.

FROM THE DESK OF: BOSS-LADY

Dear Mike,
 Thanks again.
 Everything is working out fine.
 You wouldn't know the old factory. I planted lots of flowers and turned the smokestack into a big beehive.
 The bees are happy and so am I. And there's plenty of honey.
 I'm driving up tomorrow to bring you some and to thank you personally.
                    your friend,    BOSS-LADY xx oo

P.S. Enclosed is a photo of the old place.

The next day Boss-Lady arrived in her pick-up loaded with honey. "Oh good!" said Michael Bird-Boy. "I'll bake us a honey cake."

And he did, while Boss-Lady told him all the details.

Then they had a party.

And that night Michael Bird-Boy and Boss-Lady sat among the flowers, with the white birds and watched the annual comet display.

Good night.